The Tufa Coloring Book

Illustrated by
Shoshanah Lee Marohn & **Alex Bledsoe**

Based on the stories by

The Tufa Coloring Book

Written by Alex Bledsoe

Illustrated by Shoshanah Lee Marohn

ISBN-13: 978-1535253932
ISBN-10: 1535253932

When Shoshanah Marohn suggested we do a Tufa coloring book, I was surprised; I knew that adult coloring books were now a thing, and that the medium had served series like *Game of Thrones*, *Outlander* and *Harry Potter* quite well. But those were high-fantasy tales, with vivid costumes, otherworldly settings, monsters and so forth. My Tufa novels take place in a small town in east Tennessee, in the present. Not the most visual of sources.

Yet Shoshanah, with her unique style and unbridled enthusiasm, saw nothing but striking images, and here she's created them for you to enjoy. Her style is open, simple without being crude, and always fun. You'll see her vision of the Pair-A-Dice roadhouse, the SEE ROCK CITY barn, the Widow's Tree, and other locations from the novels. And since this is a coloring book, you don't just look at them. You can put a little bit of yourself in all the drawings.

There are images from all four novels here (*The Hum and the Shiver*, *Wisp of a Thing*, *Long Black Curl* and *Chapel of Ease*) as well as the short story "The Two Weddings of Bronwyn Hyatt." There's also one preview from the upcoming fifth novel, *Gather Her Round*. And to be honest, I'm looking forward to coloring them as much as I hope you are.

Thanks so much for joining Shoshanah and me on this little jaunt through my fictional county.

With two chords and some gossip,

Alex Bledsoe

Mama done told me
Mark and 'member your tune
If you're gonna ride the night wind
In the light of the full moon

                    -Tuatha Dea, "The Hum and the Shiver"
                                        tuathadea.net

Suddenly he emerged into a clear spot bathed in bright sunlight. To the right loomed a big rectangular sign halfway up the hillside.

—Wisp of a Thing

She felt the weight of the house almost the way normal people felt the clothes against their skin. This spot had housed Overbays for longer than most could imagine, and now she was the last one.

—*Wisp of a Thing*

Janet was, even by Tufa standards, a musical prodigy, possibly on a scale with Mozart; she could play anything, had written songs and operas and even symphonies, and although she was only seventeen, she was the best picker in the county. Her all-female band, Little Trouble Girls, was a growing YouTube sensation, and as soon as they all turned eighteen, Janet planned for them to start gigging all over the southeast.

—*Gather Her Round*

Her mother was on her knees at the bottom of the yard, picking the beginnings of weeds from the dirt. Her autoharp rested on a folding chair nearby. A mockingbird flew down, perched on the chair, and pecked once at the instrument's strings.

-The Hum and the Shiver

She was a Gibson A-5 model, with two sound holes that looked like calligraphied letter *f*'s parallel to the strings. She was polished to burnished perfection except in places where the finish was worn down to the wood grain, evidence of her nearly century-long use.

-The Hum and the Shiver

Byron took out his guitar. When he looked up, John let out a long, plaintive wail from his fiddle, and Byron strummed along...

If it registered on Byron that neither of these men seemed overly concerned with the plane crash or its victims, that neither had inquired about whether Byron was injured, and that the moonshine jug never seemed to get any emptier, Byron pushed it aside... And if it seemed impossibly odd as well, out in the middle of the Tennessee woods, he'd just deal with that later, when they'd finished playing.

Unfortunately, he had no idea how long that would truly be.

-Long Black Curl

It was a long concrete building with two big wooden cutouts of dice perched at the peak. They'd been recently repainted, but the wood itself was warped, cracked, and needed to be replaced. A row of small birds sat along the top edge, and took off as we got out. A half dozen other vehicles were parked around the building, all old and worn.

-Chapel of Ease

"We're here to celebrate a life, not mourn its passing; Rayford is with the night winds now, and he sure doesn't need our tears. Let's get the music started, what do you say?"

—*Chapel of Ease*

There was indeed a little girl, no more than five or six, singing as she ran around in circles. She wore a faded little dress and no shoes, and a small puppy played at her heels.

-Long Black Curl

Fly me into the night
I wanna dance in the light of the moon
Spread my wings and take flight
Night winds are calling the tune
                    -Tuatha Dea, "The Hum and the Shiver"
                                    tuathadea.net

"Do you ever get right on the edge and think about jumping? Not because you're suicidal or anything, but just to see if you can fly?"

-*Chapel of Ease*

On the wall over the desk hung a framed cross-stitched quote attributed to William Blake:

GREAT THINGS ARE DONE WHEN MEN AND MOUNTAINS MEET

He was startled to see, not his Gmail account, but the Tufa Mysteries Web site. He forgot he'd made it his home page just before he left Kansas.

-Wisp of a Thing

Gorvens family, Cloud County, TN, 1898

No matter how fast I ran, or how many times I zigged and zagged, I heard the dog getting closer. First his paws, then his growling, then his breathing.

-Chapel of Ease

"Hey!" Guy cried. "Did you see that?"

"What?" Large Sarge asked.

"Outside the window. Something flew past."

Sarge leaned over and looked. He saw the plane's wing, the moonlight on the clouds, and the stars in the cold air. "I don't see anything."

"Maybe it was a bird," Byron said.

"At night?" Guy protested. "And it was *big*!"

"Owls are pretty big," Byron suggested.

"Do they fly this high?" Guy asked.

Before anyone could respond, the plane suddenly lurched and threw them first against the right cabin wall, then the ceiling.

-Long Black Curl

He turned the top album over and read the brief liner notes. "A new down-home sound for the uptown crowd," they proclaimed. "Rockhouse Hicks turns his banjo inside out, with a freewheeling style not seen since Bill Monroe." A quote from Roy Acuff, in large italic print, claimed Rockhouse was "the best hillbilly picker runnin' around loose."

-Wisp of a Thing

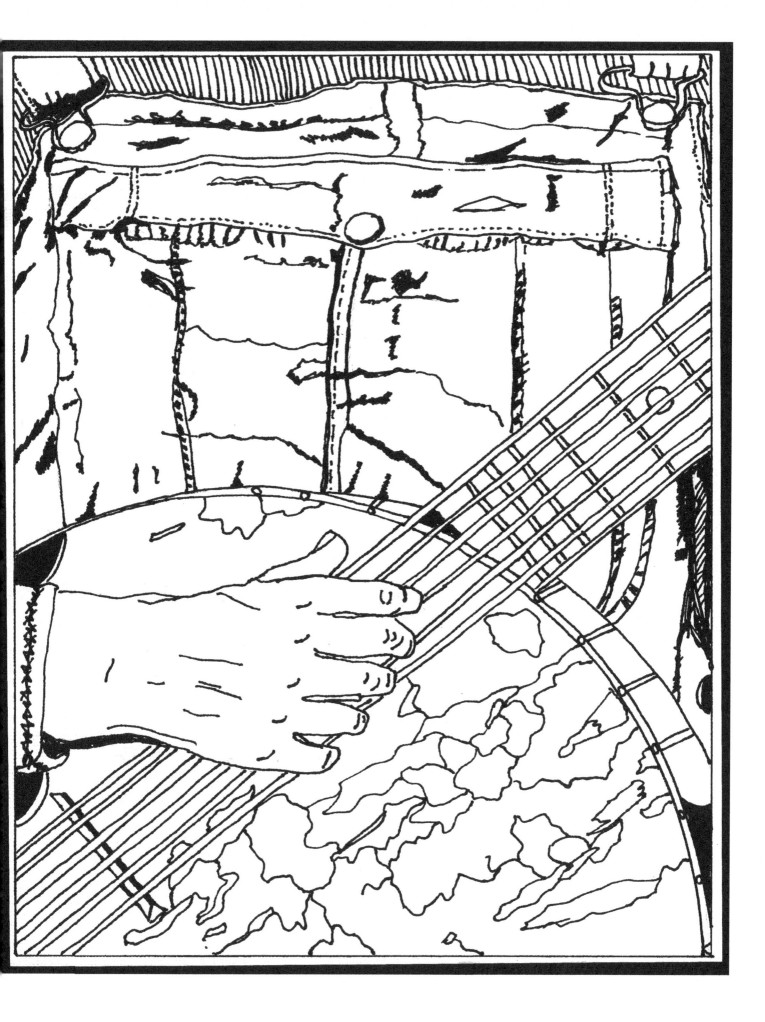

A screech owl stood on the porch rail, its tiny talons scratching against the wood. The dawn light made the tufts of its wind-ruffled feathers look jagged and bloody. The bird had a voice far out of proportion to its size, and was intimately acquainted with the night winds that guided the Tufa destiny. It was also, when seen during the day, an omen of death.

- The Hum and the Shiver

As he drove, Rob noticed something in the yard of an old shack ahead on the right. At first he thought it was one of those elaborate homemade mailboxes, fashioned into the shape of a tractor or a gas pump. Then it stepped into the road and blocked his way.

-Wisp of a Thing

The little folk quickly filed into the back two rows of pews on Bronwyn's side and had to jump or climb to get a seat. When they were settled, Bronwyn turned back to Reverend Landers.

"Sorry. They're friends of mine."
                    -"The Two Weddings of Bronwyn Hyatt"

"*The Fairy Feller's Master Stroke*," the librarian said. "It's one of our most prized pieces. And it's not the watercolor copy, either. That's in the Tate Gallery in London. This," she said with pride, "is the original."

-*The Hum and the Shiver*

"Not until the last leaf falls off the Widow's Tree."
-Wisp of a Thing

"Yes, well, how did your hunting expedition go?"

"I got what I needed." She held up the plastic baggy with the severed fingers.

"Nigel's eyes opened wide. Softly he said, "My God, are those-?"

-Long Black Curl

Tain was so beautiful, so unencumbered by societal shame or self-consciousness, that in many ways it was like seeing a goddess. He remembered in primary school they'd covered the story of the goddess Artemis and Actaeon, the unfortunate hunter who'd accidentally glimpsed her naked while she was bathing. She was so angry, she turned him into a stag, and his own hunting dogs killed him. Nigel wondered if he risked a similar fate.

-Long Black Curl

These were world-class players, and here they were in a barn in the middle of the Smoky Mountains playing just for the sheer hell of it.

-Wisp of a Thing

As he got his guitar from the trunk, he impulsively picked up a couple of rocks from the gravel road. He stuck them in his pocket without really knowing why.

-*The Hum and the Shiver*

It was something like a deer... Its head rose at least as high as mine, and it sported gigantic antlers that branched into over a dozen thick points. It was backlit by the sun, and seemed to be posing in profile for our benefit. Then it turned and stared at us with the haughty superiority I'd seen in some choreographers.

"What is that?" I whispered.

"That," C.C. said equally as softly, "is the king of the forest."

-Chapel of Ease

Tufa flight was something she could never explain to someone like him.

-The Hum and the Shiver

I had a shock I totally didn't expect: the chapel before me looked almost exactly like the one on our stage. It was larger, but the design was the same down to the lone column outside the entrance, which once supported the porch overhang. The contours of the walls, the places where major sections were missing and huge cracks rent the stone down to the foundation, were identical.

-Chapel of Ease

Then we emerged into a clearing. In the center was a small, fenced-in graveyard with perhaps a dozen headstones. Three enormous crows lifted off as we approached, their caws echoing in the silence.

-Chapel of Ease

... she rushed from room to room, lighting everything that looked like it would burn while continuing to sing.

-Long Black Curl

He flew like a badly made paper airplane, but he still flew, and although he hit the ground, it wasn't hard enough to break anything. He again knocked the wind from his lungs and lay atop a pair of protruding rocks until it returned.

When he sat up, a large black bear watched him from less than five feet away.

-Long Black Curl

... through the trees I caught glimpses of enormous letters on its roof. When we got close enough, I saw that it urged people to SEE ROCK CITY.

"What's Rock City?" I asked.

"It's a place down in Chattanooga," Gerald said. "Up on a mountain. They say you can see seven states from there."

"Is that close to here?"

"Nope. But somebody a long time ago had the bright idea of buying up roof space on barns all over the place to advertise it."

"You ever been there?"

"Naw. I got no need to see Alabama, and I've seen enough of the rest of 'em to do me for a while."

-Chapel of Ease

Made in the USA
Coppell, TX
08 September 2020